All Shapes Matter

Written By
Sreekanth Kumar
Chakra Sreekanth

Edited By
Sashi Sreekanth

Illustrated By
Chakra Sreekanth
Emily Zieroth

All Shapes Matter
Written by Sreekanth Kumar and Chakra Sreekanth
Edited by Sashi Sreekanth
Illustrations by Chakra Sreekanth and Emily Zieroth

Summary
All Shapes Matter is a story about five shapes - triangles, rectangles, squares, octagons and circles. The shapes spend their first day at elementary school learning a lot about each other and having fun. However, during recess, some of the shapes come across a problem they are unable to fix by themselves. The unfamiliar shapes who were initially shunned for being different end up coming to their aid. The shapes learn a valuable lesson that their differences can sometimes be more important than their similarities. They realize that there is value in diversity and that 'All Shapes Matter', no matter how similar or different they are.

Paperback ISBN : 978-1-7327385-0-8
Hardback ISBN : 978-1-7327385-8-4
Library of Congress Control Number: 2018910387

Published by Chakra Publishing House LLC
West Windsor, NJ 08550
chakra.publishing.house@gmail.com

Printed in the United States of America

DEDICATED TO MY NIECES & CHAKRA'S FIRST COUSINS

Dear Samyu and Saman,

I was the youngest in the family until you were born. I was the focus of the entire family, and everyone spoke about my superhero reading and writing abilities. That was until the two of you came along. I wasn't a writer anymore - your scribbles were all everyone spoke about. My emphasis on grammar and sentence construction apparently paled in comparison to anything you wrote - I am still trying to figure that one out. It would take me days to create a work of art, but it was only after you both wrote your mumbo-jumbo on top of it that it ever got noticed. I am sure just to spite me, you are going to buy this book and do the same. But remember this before you do something like that, I know your parents - you have been warned.

Stories matter a great deal to everyone, and you have inspired us to tell a story. Showing empathy through acceptance has always been in your DNA. Chakra and I couldn't have picked a better theme for our first book. It's time for your undoubtedly favorite uncle in the world and favorite cousin in the world to thank you for inspiring us. Thank you for being such an important part of our lives.

θ

MEET THE CHARACTERS

 CIRCLE

 TRIANGLE

 RECTANGLE

 SQUARE

 OCTAGON

Once upon a time in Turning Corners Elementary School, it was the first day of school for triangles, rectangles, squares, octagons and circles.

Triangles, rectangles, squares, octagons and circles had a busy first morning meeting their teachers, learning a lot and then eating lunch. After lunch, they finally heard an announcement on the school radio they were all eagerly waiting for - RECESS. All the shapes headed straight to the playground.

The squares were the first ones out. They headed straight to the swings.

The triangles, rectangles and octagons then ran over to other parts of the playground.

The triangles headed to the slide.

The rectangles headed to the monkey bars.

The octagons headed to the tunnel slide.

After playing on their own for some time, the shapes decided it was time to play with the other shapes and get to know them better.

The triangle introduced itself first. "Look at me!" said the triangle.

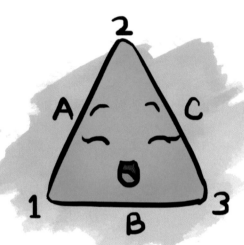

I have 3 sides and 3 corners.

I can make myself look like an arrow...

....or make myself look like a slide.

The rectangle introduced itself next. "Look at me!" said the rectangle. I have 4 sides, 4 corners and my opposite sides are equal.

I can make myself look like a flag...

...or make myself look like a food tray that we use during lunch.

The square continued with the introductions. "Look at me!" said the square. Like the rectangle, I too have 4 sides and 4 corners. In fact, I am a special type of rectangle with 4 equal sides.

I can get together with other square friends to make a rubix cube...

...or make myself look like a diamond that sparkles.

The octagon introduced itself last. "Look at me!" said the octagon. I have 8 sides and 8 corners.

I can make myself look like a trampoline...

...or look like a stop sign.

At about the time the octagons were done introducing themselves, along came two circles who excitedly asked, "Can we tell you something about us too?"

The triangles, rectangles, squares and octagons had never met a circle before and were not sure how to respond. They said...

The triangles, rectangles, squares and octagons told the circles, "we cannot play with you, you are not much fun."

The circles became very sad because of what the other shapes said. They decided to go away to a corner of the playground.

Triangles, rectangles, squares and octagons were so glad they had many sides and corners. Once the circles left, they said to each other, "since we have so many sides and corners, let's build something fun together, let's build a school bus."

Triangles, rectangles, squares and octagons came up with a plan to build the school bus.

The triangles, rectangles, squares and octagons worked hard
to build the school bus.

The hard work of the triangles, rectangles, squares and octagons paid off as they finished building the school bus. They all said, "let's take our school bus for a ride."

However, there seemed to be a problem as the school bus would not move. Try as they might, the triangles, rectangles, squares and octagons could not figure out what they were doing wrong.

Meanwhile, the circles were watching what was going on as the triangles, rectangles, squares and octagons struggled with the school bus. The circles had an idea!

The circles walked over to the school bus and said, "We can help you."

The circles went under the school bus and just like how the squares became the windows; the rectangles became the doors; the octagons became the stop signs; the circles became the wheels.

The circles started turning. The other shapes became overjoyed as their school bus started to move now.

The shapes had a lot of fun going around the playground in the school bus. All the shapes were thrilled, happy and content at what they built together during recess.

Back at recess, the triangles, rectangles, squares and octagons each had something to say to the circles.

The triangles, rectangles, squares and octagons learned something very important that day.

"It doesn't matter if you have 1 side, 2 sides, 3 sides or no sides."

"It doesn't matter if you have 1 corner, 2 corners, 3 corners or no corners."

"It doesn't matter if you can make 1 object, 2 objects, 3 objects or no objects."

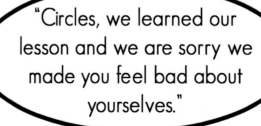

"Circles, we learned our lesson and we are sorry we made you feel bad about yourselves."

The circles accepted the apologies and forgave the triangles, rectangles, squares and octagons.

The shapes said, "It doesn't matter what shape we all come in, the only thing that matters is being nice and accepting each other for who we are. We all need different shapes – with sides or without sides, with corners or without corners."

The shapes were so happy to learn such a valuable lesson that they held hands together and shouted out – **"All Shapes Matter!"**

The End

About Chakra Sreekanth

Chakra Sreekanth (born in January 2011) is a budding American writer & illustrator of Indian origin. Chakra started working on this book in Kindergarten and at the time of publishing this book, started 2nd grade. He loves reading books, math, playing the violin and hanging out with his friends. Chakra co-wrote the book with his father, Sreekanth Kumar. Chakra's mother, Sashi Sreekanth gave the book it's title "All Shapes Matter" and was instrumental in editing, providing valuable insights & feedback on the script and illustrations. Chakra illustrated the hand-drawn pages that were subsequently illustrated to a print-ready version by co-illustrator Emily Zieroth.

Chakra's parents were inspired to put this book to fruition because of the empathy he displayed at home and school with family and friends. Chakra's choice of words, illustrations and even selection of the colors and font in this book were central to aligning the story, images and message to kids entering or already in elementary school. The following two pages provide a sample of Chakra's illustrations

Chakra's Illustrations

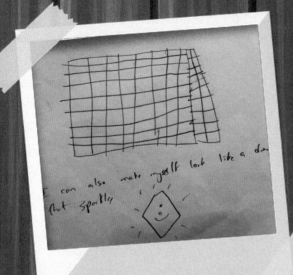

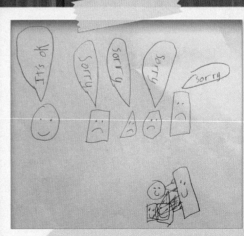

Chakra's Illustrations

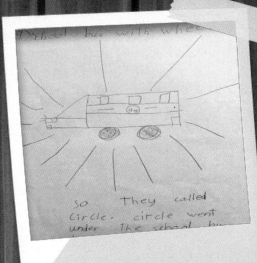

Made in the USA
Middletown, DE
04 September 2020